CROSSING LINES

Written By DC Swain
Published by Cambridge Town Press
(C) Copyright 2014 DC Swain
www.dcswain.com
ISBN 978-0-473-39468-4

Crossing Lines

By DC Swain

1

The rush of air across the back of his legs told Michael that the car had come close. But he had learned that the locals would never hit an *oyibo*, a white man. He had seen them appear to speed up to hit, or at least scare, the locals especially the children. Their begging verged on nuisance to those rich enough to own a car. Michael always gave to the children whenever he could, a few cents or food. It was why he came to Nigeria instead of university after all, to help in any way he could. But now, his time was up.

He had come to Africa to "make a difference" as he had put it to his mother while convincing her that he could take a gap year. Though having said it, he found himself disappointed for using such a clichéd tone. The brush with the local traffic made him stop and reassess his surroundings. The sun was still high on the rusting red roofs of the colonial-style buildings.

A lack of street signs made it difficult for tourists to know where they were. But Michael had learned to navigate Enugu's dusty streets. Notre Dame School was a couple of blocks behind him. The shouting of protests or civil unrest, which he had first heard this morning, was in the next street. Walking past the only travel agent in town, Michael contemplated changing his flight. He longed to spend more time in this city that fascinated and scared him at the same time. The words of his mother rang in his ears though. She told him the open-ended ticket was if he wanted to come back sooner, once he had "found himself". Her mocking tone grated on him then and now. In this moment anywhere felt more appealing than the grey, predictable days of home. His mother had not said a word to him after he decided to go.

The act of booking was Michael's first act of defiance. He saw an opportunity to escape an overly-involved mother and a father he never saw. This was his chance to be himself and find out what he wanted to be, regardless of how corny that sounded.

A tug at the base of his shirt drew Michael out of his daydream. A young boy held out his hand in the semi-pleading, semi-demanding manner they always seemed to. He wore a faded but colourful set of shorts and a threadbare t-shirt. Michael had seen this boy before and, feeling himself getting hungry, took him to the nearest café. As they rounded the corner, the yelling grew in volume. A small group of protestors stood outside the local office of All Africa Petroleum. It was one of the few modern buildings in Enugu which made it seem out of place.

Michael stopped to watch a couple of protestors chain themselves to the building entrance. Two others chanted slogans about a pipeline. The tugging at the base of his shirt reminded him that there were other more important things he should be doing. They entered a small, empty café a couple of shops down from AAP. Michael ordered a sandwich for the boy and one for himself. They sat at a table to wait, his backpack on an unsteady chair beside him. The ceiling fans of the café did little to take the edge off the heat and once again a wave of heat washed over him as another customer entered.

The customer looked how Michael imagined the hippies of the sixties looked. She was a similar age to Michael and wore a tie-dyed skirt and loose white shirt over which her mane of blond dreadlocks fell. As she ordered, Michael recognised that distinctive British accent that he hadn't heard for over a year. He found himself staring as she finished ordering and turned around, catching his gaze.

"Being a good Samaritan are we?" she said. "Er... Excuse me?" Michael stumbled over the words as he could feel himself blushing. "Feeding the street kids. Not that I'm complaining, but there are bigger issues in this place right now than poverty."

"Like what?" Michael replied, sensing the defensiveness in his own voice.

"Those AAP bastards down the road killing hundreds of people and driving thousands of others off their land for a start." She had sat down at the same table as Michael and the boy now. "You know the Chad Cameroon oil pipeline has displaced thousands to line the pockets of their greedy shareholders…" Michael's sandwich arrived with the boy's. He grabbed it and ran out the door without a word. "Boys like him have been killed too, because families refuse to move out the way of a great, polluting pipeline…" she continued as Michael's attention wandered to her shirt. The top few buttons were undone. She wasn't wearing a bra. "So it's up to people like us to tell the world what's happening here. We have to show what's happening to these poor people, being booted off their land and killed by their own government so people like you can drive daddy's range rover." The café owner put a large bag of food on the table. "Without people like the BioGuardians bringing media attention, this part of the world would be turning into a bigger corrupt pool of crap than it is already." A second bag of food arrived and the girl stood up, still talking. "We're going to show the world what's happening here, no matter what it takes. Now pick up that other bag for me."

"Excuse me?" Michael again tripped over his words, his stare broken by the order.

"Well you've been staring down my top for the last five minutes so you might as well pay for it," she said with a wink before turning on her heel and disappearing out the door. Flustered, Michael gathered his backpack and the bag of food and chased the girl out the door. She was already handing food to the group of protestors. As Michael caught up to her one of the other protestors took the bag off him and passed it round.

"So what are you actually doing here?" Michael asked her, finally able to get a word in.

"Simple," she said. "We're showing the world what this group of greedy bastards are doing to local villagers as they build the pipeline from the Doba oil fields in Chad to the Atlantic coast of Cameroon. You have no idea how many people and animals have been displaced or even killed for the sake of oil in this area. At the very least they could move the path a couple of miles to avoid needless destruction, but no, they say it costs too much."

"But aren't the BioGuardians a bit, you know, extreme?" Michael replied.

"Companies like this underestimate how much bad publicity we generate, that's all. We send footage back to various media outlets. There's no way these companies can stop us from showing what's going on."

"So why are you here and not in Chad or Cameroon?"

"Rumour has it one of the AAP bigwigs flew in from Kenya this morning. We want to let him know what we hate what's going on." Michael went to reply but noticed the girl had become distracted. "Oh crap! Get those two unchained, Gruff's coming!" she yelled. "And you better come with us too," she ordered Michael.

"Why what's happening, who's the Gruff?" Michael asked as he turned to see a group of police marching down the road towards the group, batons drawn.

"Head of the Enugu Military Police, he's bad news, now get in the damn car," she said as a small red sedan pulled up in front of them. The police were running now.

"But I'm not involved."

"You're white, of course you're involved," she replied, throwing his bag in the back seat. She grabbed his arm. Michael resisted. "Hurry up!" she screamed. The police were on them. Michael turned to explain, but all he saw was a baton coming at him.

2

The pain in Michael's face throbbed with every heartbeat. He was stiff and sore and the smell of stale canvas overwhelmed him. As he opened his eyes he saw a large African man sitting on the stretcher opposite him. "What happened, where am I?" Michael asked.

"Try to sleep. You are safe," the man replied as he got to his feet and called out of the tent. "Beth, he is awake."

Michael watched him sit back down, noticing how dark the sky was through the flap of the tent. The glow of an open fire somewhere outside lit up one side of the tent as shadows danced across it. There was a quiet murmur of talking from outside. Any breaks in conversation gave way to an empty silence.

The flap of the tent drew back and the girl from Enugu breezed in, her dreadlocks tied in a bulky ponytail following behind her.

"What part of 'get in the damn car' didn't you understand?" she asked with a smile, sitting on the stretcher beside the African man.

"I wasn't involved," Michael replied.

"That bump on your head says different. I'm Beth by the way," she said, stretching a hand out.

"Michael," he said, shaking her hand.

"And this is Jonathon," she said, nodding towards the now smiling African man. "Can I get you anything—food, water, another blanket?"

"Do you have anything for this killer headache?"

"I'll see what I can find," Beth replied and disappeared outside.

"Does she ever turn off?" Michael asked Jonathon.

"I have never seen it," Jonathon laughed as he replied. "Now get some rest."

"But where are we?" Michael said, his anxiousness evident in his voice.

"This is a BioGuardians camp in the Korup National Park, just inside the Cameroon border. You were lucky to get this far. You should thank

Beth for pulling you into my car," Jonathon replied. "You are safe."

"But, I'm supposed to be on a flight back home."

"Do not worry. We will take care of you until we can get you to an airport," Jonathon said. Michael was unsure how much he should trust Jonathon but, with no other option, he lay his head back on the stretcher.

Beth re-entered the tent with her arms full. "Here, get these into you," she said, handing him a pill box and water bottle and putting a sad-looking sandwich down beside him. "I'll look after him for now, go and get some rest," she said to Jonathon.

Michael propped himself up on an elbow and popped two of the pills in his mouth, taking a long swig from the bottle. His head began to spin so he lay back again, putting his hands over his face. He took in a deep breath and realised his parents would still be waiting for him at the airport. "Bugger," he muttered under his breath. He turned his head and looked at Beth, who was quiet for the first time since he had met her.

In this light Michael could see a small, youthful sprinkle of freckles across her nose. Her green eyes were staring at him with an amazing intensity. Even though she was silent, Michael sensed she was ready to spring at any moment. Her knees started bouncing and she seemed ill at ease with being so quiet. As Michael's gaze caught hers, she looked down at her hands, cupped over her knees.

"Who are you guys?" Michael asked. "I've seen on TV that you guys are basically lunatics."

"The BioGuardians are not lunatics, we're just passionate about the cause" Beth replied with a wry smile.

"Is Ricky Benson here?" Michael asked. Ricky Benson was the leader of the BioGuardians and, from what Michael had seen in the media, had more money than sense. "A trust fund baby with overinflated ideas of his own grandeur" Michael remembered from some past news item.

"No," Beth said, "we heard that the Army is moving up and down the pipeline construction zone clearing anyone who is in the way. We're going to meet up with Ricky tomorrow and try and film whatever's going on."

"I don't suppose you can get me back to Enugu?" Michael said. "I'm supposed to be flying home at the moment."

"Only if you want to end up in prison," Beth replied. "The Military Police are still swarming through Enugu looking for us. We can take you back in a couple of days once they leave town. The local police don't care about us."

"Why's that?" Michael asked.

"Simple," Beth replied, "the Military Police are paid by the Army, but the local police are paid a lot more by Ricky to look the other way." Michael began wondering what he had gotten himself into. "Don't worry," Beth said as she put her hand on his shoulder, "you're in safe hands. Now get some sleep."

Michael watched her get to her feet and walk out the tent. She turned to close the flap and whispered "Sleep tight." The voices outside had grown quieter and the fire, too, seemed dimmer. The throbbing in his head seemed to be easing as he stared at the roof of the tent. The medication he had taken kicked in as he closed his eyes and drifted into a deep sleep.

3

"How's the head?" Beth asked with tension in her voice. It seemed to Michael to be more out of courtesy than expecting an answer, as he emerged from the tent. A grey morning fog was hung over the campsite. The lush, dense forest made the campsite look smaller than it really was.

"Bloody sore," Michael replied while stretching his arms above his head. He watched Beth as she loaded a backpack into an old Land Rover parked beside the fire pit. She was moving with an urgency that unnerved Michael. Looking around, he noticed they were the only people left in camp.

"Where is everyone?" he asked Beth as she grabbed Michael's backpack from the tent behind him. She either hadn't heard him or didn't want to answer. "Beth? Where is everyone?" he repeated.

"Ricky called last night," she replied. "He's in Mabolo, a village about fifty miles from here." She seemed to be holding back. Michael grabbed hold of his bag as she lifted it into the Land Rover.

"What's happened, Beth?"

"They're dead." Beth sniffed hard, holding back her tears.

"Who are? Who's dead?"

"The village. Everyone in Mabolo. Ricky says the army came through last night. Almost everyone is gone."

"I'm...I'm sorry Beth."

"We have to get there. We have to help."

"But I'm not supposed to be here. I'm supposed to be at home," Michael protested.

Beth looked at him, straight through him even. Her eyes were red. Michael wondered how long she had been crying that morning. She pursed her lips, turned on her heel and proceeded to take down the tent Michael had been sleeping in. Michael watched as Beth pulled a pole from the tent so hard it left a hole in the canvas. The tent deflated itself onto Michael's stretcher inside.

"Should I take down the stretcher?" Michael asked feebly.

Beth again turned and looked at him. Michael tried to work out if she was staring more in disbelief or anger. He felt like a small boy being castigated by his mother. He looked down at his shoes. Feeling her gaze still on him, he looked back at her face. Her look had softened slightly, although it occurred to Michael that this was more likely out of grief than any abatement of the anger she was showing against him.

"Did...did you have friends in the village?" he asked.

"The BioGuardians use Mabolo as a refuel point," Beth replied. "We helped develop their new well for fresh water. In return they supply us with food and information about the pipeline and the army."

"Oh..." Michael again stared at his shoes. "I'm sorry, Beth."

"I had friends in that village, close friends," she continued. "I want to go and help them, but no, poor little English boy wants to go home."

"I'm sorry," Michael repeated, returning his gaze to his shoes. "Do you want to just leave me here?"

"You are completely thick aren't you?" Beth said. "What are you going to say if the army finds you? Or anyone round here for that matter? How will you explain being here?"

Michael didn't reply. He wanted to be out of here. It didn't matter where. Anywhere but here would be fine. Having his mother interfering with his life felt like a warm memory, rather than meddling in his dreams. Beth was still staring at him. The fog was starting to lift and Michael could feel the warmth of the morning sun on his back. "Should I grab the stretcher?" Michael asked again, hopeful that any sort of activity would distract Beth.

"Just get in the car," Beth replied. She turned back to the tent and dragged the stretcher out before taking it apart. Michael watched her for a brief moment before staring at his feet again, hands in his pockets. Beth ignored him, folding up the stretcher and putting it in the back of the Land Rover. As Beth went back to take the rest of the tent down, Michael got into the passenger seat of the Land Rover. He slouched down in the front seat as the sun broke through the fog.

Beth finished loading the tent, got into the driver's seat and, without a word to Michael, drove down a track into the forest.

4

Michael braced himself against the door as Beth took yet another corner at a pace that had him thinking they wouldn't be coming out the other end. The trees on either side of the track reached out and touched each other, creating a tunnel through which sunlight filtered down. Beth had stopped crying but hadn't looked at Michael since they left camp. He was relieved that this meant her gaze was on the track, but at the same time felt like he was being treated unfairly. He hadn't wanted any of this – he was supposed to be on his way home.

They briefly broke free from the tunnel of trees. Water sprayed as they surging through a small stream, before hurtling back into the forest on the other side. "Beth," Michael asked, "don't you think you should slow down a bit?" Beth turned and looked at him. The speed they were travelling didn't seem to change. She was still staring at him. "Beth!!!" Michael yelled at her this time, keeping his own gaze forward. She turned her head back in time to take the next bend, bouncing roughly on a log as they cut the next corner.

The bush overhead seemed to be getting thicker when Michael found himself squinting in bright sunlight as they broke free of the bush and raced across a plain of yellowed tussock grass. The plains appeared to reach out to the horizon in front of them and to the base of far off mountains on either side. The sky was a pale blue, stretching to soft white clouds over the mountains. He relaxed as the track changed from a four-wheel drive route to a worn dirt and gravel road. The change in road only seemed to make Beth drive faster.

Michael watched a group of large black birds with pink beaks take off. The birds flew in the same direction as the car, before peeling off and heading towards the mountains. In front of them, where the road met the horizon, he could see a dark shape coming into view.

He glanced at Beth and could see that her look had softened, but she still showed no interest in talking to Michael. The shape in the distance had taken on the definite look of a small building.

As they approached, Beth slowed. Michael could see the building was set back from a T-junction, where the road they were on met a wider, two-lane road.

The small building was built from a dark wood with a red or – Michael guessed – rusted, corrugated iron roof. Someone was coming out of the building as Beth steered into a makeshift car park in front of the building. A sign in front read "Korup National Park – Ranger Station".

"Welcome, Beth," the man beamed as he approached the Land Rover. Michael was glad for the interaction with someone else. Beth's spirits seemed to lift upon seeing him and she got out of the Land Rover and into the open arms of the man. Michael could tell she was crying softly into him as he offered his free hand to Michael. "I am Peter, the ranger for Korup."

"Michael," he replied, shaking his hand, the pressure of Peter's handshake taking him slightly by surprise. Peter towered over Michael. His arm seeming like a thick black snake, constricting around Beth as she wiped her eyes against the tan of Peter's ranger shirt.

"Come," Peter ordered, still smiling as he turned towards the building, "let's get this one calmed down."

5

The heat from the stove bit at Michael's knuckles as he put the kettle on the cast iron element. He had taken charge of tea-making. Peter was preoccupied, rushing to put away papers from his desk to a filing cabinet. Beth had collapsed into the only comfortable-looking chair, high backed and faded, beside the door they had come in. A slowly turning ceiling fan was overhead. Michael watched it wobble through a couple of revolutions before gazing out the window opposite Beth.

The eave of the roof dropped low enough that Michael couldn't see the sky from his vantage point. He moved away from the stove, trying to find somewhere—anywhere—cooler. He walked in front of the window; glancing back briefly at Beth. She had now closed her eyes, resting her head against the back rest. He looked back out the open window. Here he could feel the air being sucked in the window and out the main door behind him.

The plains stretching off into the distance appeared lifeless under the high sun. Peter had joined Michael at the window. "This breeze is good, no?"

Peter asked, wiping sweat from his bald head with a bright, white handkerchief. "It's a welcome relief," Michael replied.

An old Land Rover was parked out the back. Its canopy appeared freshly patched, and "Korup Ranger" had been stencilled in black on the khaki paint of the door. Above the rear mudguard was a lion, crudely painted in bright yellow and orange, with "King of the Jungle" underneath it.

"So are you king of the jungle?" he asked, nodding towards the Land Rover.

"Well my daughter thinks so," Peter laughed as he replied. He looked at Beth, who appeared to have drifted off to sleep, before looking back at Michael.

"This is a dangerous place, Michael." Peter's tone had changed, his voice low and steady. "What are you doing with them?"

"With whom?" Michael replied.

"The BioGuardians," Peter whispered back. "They are trouble; you should not be here."

"I didn't plan on it," Michael replied. "It's not like I had a choice." Peter stared at him, but Michael struggled to read what the stare was supposed to mean. "I want to help those people though, in the village that got shot."

"Just trust me, Michael," Peter said as he put his giant hands on Michael's shoulders. "The first chance you have, get back to Nigeria. Go home."

Michael stopped to think. He wanted to be home, or at least out of this situation. Beth's speech to him that morning wandered through his mind. Something told him he had to help.

"Do you hear what I am saying?" Peter asked, looking nervously back to Beth.

"But what if I can help?" Michael asked, imitating Peter's hushed tones.

"Helping the BioGuardians is a very dangerous thing Michael. They are taking on big money here and I'm not sure they can stop the build, or even change its route for that matter. There is too much money at stake."

"But what about Ricky Benson?" Michael replied, trying to convince himself to stay. "He seems to always be in the news. Surely he can generate enough publicity about what's going on?"

"He is the worst of the lot," Peter replied, pausing to let the words sink in. "Let me help you Michael. I can take you back to the border. If we leave soon we can get you back by nightfall."

It dawned on Michael that he now had a chance to escape. He looked at Beth asleep in the chair. She seemed calm, especially compared to earlier that morning. The raw emotion she had shown that morning had an effect on Michael.

"I want to stay," he said. "I want to help."

"Michael, take my advice," Peter whispered. "The BioGuardians, they always leave the keys in their vehicles, just in case. When you change your mind, take one and head back the way you came. Do you understand?"

Beth stirred on the other side of the room as Michael slowly nodded. She opened her eyes and looked at the two men. "What are you two talking about?" she asked through a yawn.

"I was just telling Michael this is a dangerous place," Peter responded.

"Nonsense," she replied. "Besides, he is a brave boy. I'm sure he can handle himself." Beth winked at Michael, but all he could muster in return was a nervous smile. The kettle started to whistle on the stove. It was a saviour from what was about to become a tricky conversation.

6

"Right, break's over," Beth said as she took Michael's empty cup out of his hand. "We've got to load up." She led Michael out the door with Peter following closely behind. On the end of the building was a small crudely-erected storage locker. As Peter unlocked the padlock and swung open the door, Michael could see it was full of bottled water, tinned food, camouflage gear and boxes marked with a red cross—medical supplies.

"Here, packhorse," Beth said, smiling, as she handed a box of bottled water to Michael. While she was smiling again, Michael could still see the redness around her eyes from her earlier tears. He studied her face while she worked with Peter to work out what they needed. He thought about Peter's warning, but was sure Beth would keep her word to get him out of here. She had looked after him so far, but a small doubt still lingered.

Beth loaded another box into his arms and gave him a perplexed look as he stood still, looking at her. "Feeling strong enough for a third box are you?" she asked.

"No," Michael replied, snapping out of his daze. "I was remembering what happened last time I carried something for you." Beth stopped and turned towards him, squaring up to look him straight in the eye. "What are you trying to say?" she replied, struggling to contain a cheeky smirk.

"I don't feel like getting another headache," Michael smiled back. "And what are you carrying?" Beth began to laugh until Peter shoved a box into her arms.

"This," Peter said, "is for you, packhorse number two. And the truth is the biggest danger round here is your driving." Michael laughed as Beth shouldered him out the way. She looked back with a grin, before continuing with the boxes around the corner and towards the Land Rover.

"I mean it Michael, be careful," Peter again lowered his voice as he spoke to Michael. "Now let's get these in the truck," he said, carrying a couple of boxes past Michael.

In short time they had loaded a good quantity of food, water and medical supplies into the back of the Land Rover. Beth lead the three of them back to the storage locker. "I think we're done for now." As Peter went to shut the door on the storage locker, Michael pointed at the camouflage gear. "What about some of that?" Peter and Beth laughed.

"You know what this is Michael?" Peter replied. "This is Army uniform. I don't think you want to be caught wearing that."

"I just thought that since most of my clothes are already on their way back home..." Michael's voice drifted off as he realised what he was saying.

"You are not the only ones who get supplies here, Michael. The Army knows exactly what they have here; down to the last can," Peter said. "I can only give you what is marked as supplies for the tourists. Now come, you must get going to get to Mabolo before sundown. You don't want to be travelling at night."

Peter escorted Beth and Michael back to the Land Rover. "Good luck my friends, stay safe." Beth hugged him and whispered into his ear. Michael caught a soft "thank you" from her, before she bounced into the driver's seat. Peter extended a hand to Michael, "Stay safe."

Michael released the grip of their handshake first and went around the Land Rover, climbing in the passenger's door. He remained silent as Beth steered them out of the car park and back onto the seemingly endless road that had brought them here.

Staring at the dark green mountains fading into the distance, Michael's mind was heavy with Peter's words and thoughts of home. For the first time in months he actually missed it. But this was his chance. He had told his mother that he wanted to come here to change and he was positive helping the BioGuardians would do exactly that. As he pondered his decision, he was aware that Beth had said something. "Sorry, I was miles away," he said. "What was that?"

"Dust storm," Beth replied, nodding ahead of them. At the point where the crisp light blue of the sky met the horizon was a cloud of dust, moving across the plains, turning the horizon a deep shade of red.

7

The red cloud climbed higher in the sky as they approached. The winds picked up the earth and threw it into the sky, forming soft peaks at one moment and violent swirls the next. Michael watched as the local wildlife retreated across the plains. The safety of the mountains, stood a tall, dark green in the distance. The colours of this country still amazed Michael. The sky a big, empty blue dominating everything and blanketing the darkest greens of the forests. The pale green, almost white, of the tussock grassed plains poking through the rich orange-red of the earth.

Beth had taken the pressure off the accelerator as they neared the wall of dust. Michael loosened his grip on the door handle. While the dust of Enugu had often swirled around the school, Michael had never felt this exposed to its effects. Although he was, at the very least, glad because it meant Beth had slowed down.

"At least the road's straight," Michael said. "How far off is Mabolo?"

"Another couple of hours," Beth replied, "hold on." The wall of dust had reached them and began scratching at the windscreen. She slowed a little more, to a speed that Michael almost found bearable. The winds rocked the Land Rover, gently at first, and then with a violent shudder. Beth fought with the steering wheel to keep them steady on the road. Michael repeated the words "at least the road's straight" to himself. He tried to stay calm as he was able to see less and less of the road in front of them.

"How big are these normally—" Michael asked. Before he could finish they burst back into bright sunlight, back to careering across the plains. As he looked in the wing mirror to see what they were leaving behind, he felt a massive thud. Jolting forward, his seatbelt pulling tight across his chest and lap. He felt winded as he realised they had come to a complete and sudden stop. They were bonnet first into a small bank on the side of the road. He looked over at Beth who had gone pale and was looking in the wing mirror on her side of the Land Rover.

"What the hell was that?"

A steady stream of steam, or was it smoke, rose from a gap where the bonnet had been flush with the side panel of the Land Rover. Michael nudged his door with his shoulder, the top opening slightly before springing closed again. A second harder shoulder and the door sprang open and wedged against the bank. He eased himself out of the seat and stood slowly, stretching himself out to make sure he was in one piece.

He looked back up the road and saw Beth, crouching over something on the road. "I'm OK by the way!" he shouted back to her, as the dust storm seemed to increase the speed of its retreat away from them. "What is it anyway?" he asked. "What did we hit?" As he walked closer he could see the tan hide of some sort of antelope. Michael had never been very good at telling the different species apart. "Is it dead?" he asked, in a softer, more reverent tone as he reached Beth's side.

"Not quite," Beth replied. "We need to put it out of its misery." Beth stood and headed back towards the Land Rover. Michael crouched over the beast. He watched the rapid rise and fall of its chest and the blood in the corner of its mouth. It was a direct contrast to its natural elegance. The beast's front legs twitched in an unsteady pace—running. Its rear half was still, limp. Its gaze caught Michael's as Beth returned to his side. He felt trapped in its stare until he realised Beth was holding a rifle. "Good bye my friend, I'm sorry," she said, before putting the rifle against its head and pulling the trigger.

The shot had made Michael jump. He stepped back, looking at the beast and back to Beth who was walking back towards the Land Rover. "Was that really necessary?" he asked. He knew full well the creature needed to be put down, but felt shocked at the lack of ceremony surrounding it.

"It was in pain," Beth replied, putting the rifle back in the Land Rover. "We had to do it."

"I know," Michael replied, "but wasn't there a better way to do it?"

Beth paused and looked at Michael. "Not really." Michael looked away sheepishly. He knew she was right, but still wasn't comfortable with how it had happened.

"So what do we about the truck?" he asked, wanting to change the subject, but unable to stop himself from stealing a glance back at the dead creature.

"The front axle's cracked, so we need to unload," Beth replied, watching Michael staring at the creature. "Sometimes we do what we do, because it is necessary," she said softly. "It may not be nice, but we do what we have to."

Unloading the truck seemed to take twice as long as loading it. Beth directed Michael that everything they took off the truck had to be put out of sight from the road. They unloaded in silence, piling all the stores in a rut behind a small bank a few metres from the edge of the road. When just Beth and

Michael's backpacks remained in the Land Rover, Beth offered Michael a bottle of water. "And now we hope this works," she said, removing a satellite phone from under the driver's seat.

Michael sat against the bank, enjoying the small shadow cast by the Land Rover in the late afternoon sun and making sure he couldn't see the antelope. As he sat down he could finally feel how fast his heart was beating and how dry his mouth felt. He sipped the water and turned, lying on his stomach to watch the dust storm running for the mountains. Beth sat down beside him, taking a swig from a water bottle of her own, before trying the satellite phone. "Now this could be an issue," she said.

"What's that?" Michael replied, sitting up to see Beth holding the satellite phone. Turning it in her hands, Beth showed Michael a hole where the battery should have been.

8

"Now what?" Michael asked, anxious at the sight of the battery-less satellite phone.

"We wait," Beth replied. "Ricky and the others know we are coming; if we don't make it on time they'll come looking. We've got enough supplies to stay comfortable until then."

Michael rolled back on to his stomach, gazing at nothing in particular in the distance. He felt the heat of the sun on his legs where they stretched out from the shadow of the Land Rover.

Beth sat in the sun, her skin reflecting its warmth at Michael. She took a sip of water and stared off in the opposite direction. While Michael enjoyed the silence and opportunity to reflect on his situation, Peter's words weighed on his mind. He felt Beth getting fidgety beside him—he guessed that this sort of silence was a rarity for her. He played with a strand of thick yellow grass between his fingers, rolling it across his palms.

Beth took another sip of water before turning to him. "So, I never did ask you what you're doing here."

"Waiting for rescue," he replied, smiling.

"I know that," Beth replied, playfully slapping him on the thigh. "Why Africa? You don't strike me as a natural born explorer."

"I'm not," Michael replied. "I just didn't want to go to university, to be stuck behind a desk for the rest of my life." He stopped playing with the grass and turned to face Beth. "I guess, I just want to be part of something that isn't planned by my parents. So I came to the last place they would think of going and, believe it or not, I actually enjoyed helping teach."

"I think we all want to leave a mark," Beth replied. "It's how I ended up here. I saw what the BioGuardians were doing and thought—that's me. I can do something that actually matters."

"I guess so," Michael said, "but is it actually worth it? People are being killed and you think you can stop it?"

"We will," Beth replied, "I know we will. Ricky has a plan and the whole world will see what's happening here. We can't displace thousands of people for a bit of oil. Ricky says we can stop it. Or at the very least have them go around villages and conservation areas, instead of ploughing straight through the middle of them."

"But what if you get hurt?" Michael asked, admiring Beth's passion for what she was doing, but anxious about her faith in Ricky. He'd read the papers and never thought anyone would be able to put faith in someone so outspoken, so radical.

"There are some things you have to take a risk for," Beth said. "I mean, you could get run over crossing the road on your way to work behind a desk. Or you could get hurt out here...which one would you rather?"

"I guess so," Michael replied, more out of courtesy, given that right now being stuck behind a desk didn't seem like such a bad idea. "You're really passionate about this, aren't you?"

"You have to be passionate about something," Beth replied, "otherwise why do anything? I can't think of anything more deserving than the world we live in to be passionate about."

Michael looked back to the mountains, then down at the grass in front of him. "Peter said you guys are trouble," he said, waiting for a reaction. When it didn't come he turned to look at Beth, who was staring along the road. A vehicle was coming towards them, a trail of dust kicked up into the air, floating and then diluting itself down. "Is that our rescue party?" he asked.

Beth watched the vehicle for a while longer, trying to make out what it looked like, before replying "I hope so."

9

Michael could sense Beth tensing up as the ute approached. They could now see that it wasn't the rescue they had hoped for. An official-looking emblem was on the side of the ute and several people were standing in the back. As Michael looked behind them he could see another vehicle coming into sight.

"Soldiers?" Michael asked. He stood and folded himself in against the Land Rover, hoping they would drive on by.

"Police," Beth replied. "Not as bad as soldiers, but still not what we want to see." Her voice sounded strained as she stood beside him. "Hopefully that's not more of them," she said, also looking at the other vehicle. "Do whatever they say and don't look them in the eye, don't challenge them."

"I just want to get the hell out of here," Michael replied.

"We'll get you home," Beth reassured him. "I promised, remember?" She took his hand and squeezed it softly.

The ute pulled in beside them and before it even came to a complete stop four men in navy uniforms jumped off the back. Machine guns in their hands, they yelled at Beth and Michael to put their hands behind their heads.

"What are two foreigners doing out here?" the man in the driver's seat boomed at them through his open window. Beth stayed silent, and Michael followed suit. He had decided that following Beth's advice might be prudent this time. The man in the ute opened his door and marched between the four others. His portly frame making him look comical against the tall, lithe officers surrounding him. He pushed his sunglasses up to his forehead and walked up to Michael, who could smell the tang of tobacco on his breath.

"I said, what are you doing here?" the man again bellowed, and Michael was sure he could hear the man's voice echoing. Again Michael stayed silent.

"We're just tourists," Beth answered the man, keeping her eyes to the ground. Michael snuck a look at the four officers who seemed to be holding their weapons awkwardly. The man hadn't taken his eyes off Michael, who quickly returned his eyes to the ground.

The man leaned in to Michael. "You always let your woman do your talking?" One of the officers laughed. Michael looked at the man, his forehead sweaty and his eyes yellowing at the edges.

"She's not my woman," Michael replied. "She's just a friend I'm travelling with."

"Then maybe she could be my woman," the man said. "What do you think, my darling?" He took his attention from Michael to Beth, who still kept her gaze firmly at the ground. "Please," she said, "we're just travelling through."

Michael again looked at the four officers who had focussed their attention on Beth. He could see over their shoulders. The other vehicle coming their way, another ute, was getting closer.

"Then in that case," the man turned his attention back to Michael, "show me your documents." Michael kept his gaze down again, not sure what exactly to do.

"They're in the glove box," Beth again replied for him.

"You're actually her woman, aren't you?" the man said, poking a stumpy finger into Michael's chest. Michael kept in control of himself, not reacting, staring at the ground. The man looked him up and down and yelled something in a language Michael couldn't quite pick. One of the officers went around the other side of the Land Rover, opened the door and searched the glove box.

"Take my advice, boy," the man whispered in Michael's ear, "don't let your woman do the talking." As he finished he raised his hand and slapped Michael across the face. The sting of the slap wasn't too bad, but the shock of it buckled Michael's knees. He tried not to react and straightened himself, keeping his eyes to the ground.

He saw the hands of the officer who had been collecting their papers and became panicked. Beth, or someone back at camp, had removed his passport from his pack and put it in the glove box with Beth's. The passport itself didn't worry Michael. It was the blue cardboard folder protruding from the middle of it that he needed. Inside that folder was his ticket to fly home. From Enugu. How was he going to explain being in Cameroon when he was supposed to have already flown out of Nigeria?

He could hear the second vehicle nearing them.

The man opened Beth's passport first. He held it open by her face, looking from the photo to Beth's dusty face. "You are a pretty girl when you are clean," he snapped at her. He turned his attention back to her passport, rifling through the pages. "You have been here for a month?" he questioned. Beth nodded in reply. "When are you leaving?" he asked, adding "The sooner the better I should think, no?" before Beth could answer. Beth again nodded, keeping her eyes down.

"And now, woman, let's have a look at yours," the man said, turning back towards Michael and opening his passport. He again studied the photo page of the passport against Michael's face. As he began to leaf through the pages, Michael swallowed nervously. "When did you enter Cameroon?" the man asked, flicking through the passport for a second time. Michael didn't answer. He couldn't. He looked straight at his shoes, not daring to move. "I said, when did you come here?" the man demanded. "You have no entry stamp. When did you get here?"

The slap this time was a lot harder and Michael dropped to the ground. A patch of red earth seemed to be shooting heat straight through him. He could hear the other vehicle pulling over and hurried talking between the officers. He looked up to see the man pointing his pistol straight at him. "How did you get here?" he said again with anger in his voice. "Why are you here?"

Michael put his hand up, partly to block the low sun shining into his eyes and partly, somewhat naively, to shield himself from the pistol.

10

"What's the problem here?"

It was a new voice, definitely American, and one that sounded vaguely familiar. Michael looked in the direction it had come from. A short man with a crop of curly red hair was getting out of the ute that had pulled in, its engine still running. Michael recognised him from news he had seen before—Ricky Benson had arrived.

Ricky strutted between the officers. He either didn't see or didn't care that they all had their weapons trained on him. He stood between the man and Michael. "Captain Kasolo, I haven't seen you for awhile," Ricky said, extending his hand. Kasolo took Ricky's hand awkwardly, shaking it, while trying to keep the pistol aimed at Michael.

"This one does not have any entry papers," Kasolo said, shaking his pistol to point at Michael.

"I'm sure it's just a mistake at the border," Ricky said. "An administration issue." Michael could see Ricky put his hand in his pocket and pull out a thick envelope. He handed it to Kasolo and glanced back at Michael, winking before looking back at Kasolo.

"I think you are possibly correct," Kasolo replied. "Our border guards can be a little forgetful." He stuffed the envelope into his pocket, handed the passports to Ricky and barked at the officers to get back in the ute. He appeared to Michael to be in a hurry to get out of there. Michael started to get up, but he felt Ricky's hand on his shoulder. "Wait till they're gone." He watched as Kasolo and the officers reversed back onto the road and sped off towards the ranger's station, a plume of dust in their wake.

Ricky helped Michael as he pulled himself up from his knees, dusting himself off. "So you're the one with the headache from Enugu?" Ricky asked, taking Michael's hand and shaking it.

"Yeah," Michael replied, "I'm Michael."

"And I'm Ricky," he said, lowering his sunglasses to peer over the top of them, "but I am guessing you already knew that." He smiled, pushed his sunglasses back up to his eyes and turned on his heel to turn his attention to Beth.

Michael looked back at the ute Ricky had arrived in and saw a familiar face getting out of the driver's side. "You seem to always be finding trouble," Jonathon said, smiling at Michael.

"It seems that way," Michael replied. "Thanks for the rescue."

"You can thank Ricky, not me," Jonathon said. "He wanted to come out early—he had heard there were a lot of police in the area at the moment."

"Well," Michael shrugged his shoulders, thanks anyway."

"Can we get that thing going?" Jonathon asked, nodding towards the Land Rover.

"I don't think so," Michael replied, "it's crashed pretty bad. We put the supplies over that bank." Jonathon walked in the direction Michael had indicated. As Michael followed he saw Ricky in deep conversation with Beth. They were whispering, but their body language told Michael that something was wrong. Beth seemed to be the one at fault.

The conversation continued as Michael and Jonathon loaded the ute with the supplies. Michael watched as Ricky seemed to be berating Beth. Ricky looked up and seemed to catch Michael's stare, which he quickly averted to the ground in front of him. "We'll be there to help shortly," Ricky called out to them. Michael couldn't tell if the tone in Ricky's voice was a genuine offer of help, or a subtle hint that their conversation was private.

With the last of the supplies loaded, Jonathon got into the driver's seat of the ute and started the engine. It was a hint to Ricky and Beth, Michael guessed, who were still in discussion. Michael got into the passenger's seat and watched them in the wing mirror.

"Do you know what you are heading for in Mabolo?" Jonathon asked.

"Not really," Michael replied, "I know a lot of people are hurt."

"A lot of people are dead," Jonathon corrected him. "There are a lot of people there that need our help, but it is not a nice place to be right now."

"I'm ready to help," Michael said. "I want to help." He thought back to the conversations he had with his mother and then with Beth. This was his chance to do something that mattered.

Ricky and Beth got into the back seat of the ute from opposite sides. The distance between them seemed to Michael to be a little too big. They each seemed to compress themselves against the doors to increase the space as much as possible. Jonathon turned them back onto the main road, towards the horizon and the massacre in Mabolo.

11

The forest at the base of the distant mountains seemed to be racing them as they sped along the dusty road towards Mabolo. Michael had dozed off for what seemed like a brief moment, only to wake and see that the sun had lowered itself. The forest that they had been running parallel to was now converging on them. His head hurt and the incessant drone of the engine seemed to cross between soothing and aggravating him. He looked back and saw that Beth too had fallen asleep against the slightly open window.

Ricky had a notebook open and was writing; he looked up and smiled. "Good sleep?" Michael nodded and looked back in front of them as the forest from either side met, turning the road into a form of tunnel. The brief glimpses of light Michael saw through the leafy canopy had lost the glare of earlier in the day and he felt himself shiver.

A side road appeared through a hole in the jungle wall that Jonathon eased them onto. They left behind the smooth red main road and onto a track that had once been carved through the earth, but was now being reclaimed by roots and vines. A fresh dampness entered Michael's nostrils as they wobbled along the track. Michael heard Beth stir in the back and he could sense Ricky and Jonathon tensing up. *Mabolo must be close*, he thought to himself.

The track entered Mabolo by rounding a small hut. It was constructed of mud bricks contained in a wooden frame, with a thick mat of straw and grasses making do for a roof. It stood showing little evidence of what Beth had told Michael about that morning. Though he realised he wasn't exactly sure of what to expect. As they turned in front of the hut Michael was able to get a much better view of the village. It was a collection of huts. Identical in construction to the first, built along a bank of deep red earth that sloped down to a murky yellow-brown river. The far bank was a towering wall of jungle.

A small group of people were ferrying supplies from utes into two of the larger huts. Michael could see smoke rising from a clearing down the far end of the village. "Welcome to Mabolo," Jonathon said softly, as if not to disturb something in the air around them. "The two huts over there have the survivors in them. Most of the dead have been taken to the pyres down the far end." He nodded towards where the smoke was emanating from. "We need to put all these supplies into that first hut," he continued. "That's where we will sleep tonight too."

Michael watched as a group of people emerged from one of the huts containing the survivors, carrying what looked like a large sack towards the far end of the village. As Michael got out of the ute he could see that it wasn't a sack at all, rather the body of a man, hanging limp.

The movement of the supplies distracted Michael until a gentle breeze blew from the far end of the village carrying with it the acrid smell of burnt flesh from the pyres. He dry retched and struggled, pulling himself together, trying to focus on the thought that there were people here in a lot worse state than him.

"Can you give me a hand with these?" Ricky asked Michael, indicating to the two cardboard boxes left in the ute. Michael watched Beth and Jonathon head into one of the huts and wished he was with them. Ricky had a way about him that made Michael feel uneasy. Reluctantly, he picked up the last box and followed Ricky down through the village. He was able to catch brief glimpses of the few occupants of each hut, every one of them showing shock, grief and anger.

The smell became a stench as Ricky and Michael reached the clearing at the end of the village. At least a dozen fires were burning, sending a thick plume into the air. Wails echoed off the surrounding trees as men and women grieved for those lost. Michael looked away from the fires, turning his head to see an unlit pyre. Wood was stacked over the body of a child wearing a deep blue shirt, a congealed, bloody mess where part of his chest should have been. Michael turned away, dropping the box, and vomited into the bushes at the side of the clearing.

He turned to see someone setting light to the pile and he knew he had to get out of there. He retched again. With nothing left to come out, he half ran, half stumbled, back through the village, stopping only when he reached the ute. Michael fumbled around the ignition, feeling the keys but unable to grasp them. He seized upon the end of the key and gave it a sharp twist, sending a load roar from the engine. He could see in the wing mirror that Beth and Jonathon had come out of the hut, trying to see what was going on.

Michael pushed the clutch in and felt yet another wave of nausea come over him. He threw the door open and fell out onto the ground, unable to control his stomach, feeling nothing but the sting of bile coating the back of his throat.

The engine of the ute cut out and he felt an arm around him. "Shhh..." Beth whispered into his ear, "You'll be okay." Michael realised he was sobbing, large tears rolling down his face. He collapsed into Beth, burying his face in her lap as she sat beside him, softly rubbing his back. Michael could hear her talking, but the words weren't registering with him. He had to hide. To get away from that place.

Michael let himself go limp as he felt an arm go around his shoulders and one under his knees. Jonathon lifted him with ease, carrying him to a hut and laying him on a stretcher. The smell of old canvas was some relief to Michael as he felt a coarse blanket being pulled over him. "I'll take the first shift," Beth said, escorting Jonathon back out of the hut.

Michael closed his eyes, desperately hoping for the escape of sleep, but was only able to find the image of that dead child. A young boy. Dead. And over what? Michael knew this village lay in the path of the pipeline, but surely it wasn't worth killing over?

"Can I get you anything?" Beth asked as Michael reopened his eyes.

"Have you got anything to erase my memory?"

"Unfortunately, no," Beth said, running her hand down his shoulder. "It doesn't get any easier I'm afraid. This isn't the first time something like this has happened."

"But why do they have to burn them? Can't they bury them?" Michael asked, the vision of the fires and the dead boy racing through his head again.

"Animals disturb graves," Beth replied matter-of-factly. "They've been doing it this way for hundreds of years. The only alternative is to cover graves with piles of rocks, and there aren't too many rocks around here."

Michael stared off into nothing while Beth played with her shoelaces.

"How can this happen?" Michael's croaky voice broke the silence.

"Greed," Beth replied, "that's pretty much it. This place lies bang smack in the middle of the pipeline route. If they were to go round, it would cost a fortune to cut straight through the forest. They take the easiest and cheapest route and just get rid of whatever is in the way."

Michael rubbed his forehead, trying to take it all in. He wanted to cry, vomit and scream all at once, while at the same time satisfied that he had resolved to stay on. "How do we stop it?"

"We keep trying," Beth replied. "Ricky said he has a plan." Beth's voice trailed off and she looked away from Michael.

"Do you need to call home?" she asked softly, offering a satellite phone from a box of supplies across the hut.

Michael thought about calling home and about what he had seen today. While he needed to hear something familiar and safe, he also felt the need to stay and to help. And how would his parents help him get out of here anyway? He shook his head at Beth. "Not yet."

"I'll get you some fluids," she said, rising to her feet. At the doorway, she turned to look back at him. "You'll be okay."

The light coming through the doorway faded to a soft pink and then a flickering orange. Michael could see through his half-closed eyes that the afternoon had drifted into evening. He thought again about calling home, but then he had come to Africa to help people, and this might be his chance. He hoped that the flickering light he could see wasn't from the pyres, but the new smell in the air told him that food was being cooked.

12

Michael wasn't sure how long he had been in his half asleep state. Beth hadn't returned and he felt his tongue sticking to an acidic paste on the top of his mouth. He rolled off the stretcher and crawled across the hut to a box of water bottles. The first sip provided some relief in lubricating his mouth but the taste, although diluted, remained.

He eased himself to his feet, bracing against a wall while his balance regathered. Pulling a blanket from the stretcher, he wrapped it around his shoulders. Stooping low to walk under the doorway, he shuffled into the cool of the evening. The group by the fire didn't appear to notice him and the soft sound of their chatter merged with the crackle of the fire and movement of the forest.

Shuffling towards the group, Michael took another sip from the water bottle and grimaced again from the taste as he swallowed. "You are having a rough time, my friend," a voice called from the hut Michael was passing. Jonathan's smile appeared to glow in the dimly lit hut. "Come, sit, let me introduce you to Ajani," he said, patting at the ground beside him.

As Michael entered the hut he could see who Jonathan had been gesturing at. On the stretcher beside him an old man lay under a blanket, his greying hair looking dirty and crusted with blood from a cut across his forehead. Jonathan wiped his forehead while the old man spoke softly. Jonathan gave a brief reply and the man smiled at Michael.

"Ajani knew my father," Jonathan said. "He says he remembers when he was your age and the first white man came to Mabolo. That was a good man. Not like the men building the pipe." Michael lowered himself down beside Jonathan. "Do not worry Michael," he smiled. "I have told him you are a good man."

"You grew up around here?" Michael replied. "It's a beautiful place."

"I was born in Nkumbe, down the river. It was a beautiful place, but the pipeline, it is destroying it. Our land, my family's land, Ajani's land, is being taken."

"What will happen to them?"

"They will move on. They are strong people, but the land where we grew our crops, hunted our food, it is taken. They will have to start again." Jonathan's voice trailed off. "That is why we must stop the pipeline, so my children and their children can grow on the land where I grew."

"So that's why you joined the BioGuardians?"

"Yes. Mr Ricky has come to help my people, so I will do whatever I can to help him."

"Is there anything I can do?" Michael replied.

Jonathon reached into a bag at his feet and pulled out a small video camera. "Take this," he said, "and document what you see." Michael took the camera, turned it on and filmed Jonathon as he sat with Ajani. "We all carry cameras. Mr Ricky said it's the best way to get our story to the world. We film what we see and he sends it off."

Michael observed through the viewfinder as Jonathon offered a sip of water to Ajani. The old man's eyes looked tired, yet somehow strong in the soft light. He whispered a few soft words of what Michael presumed were thanks to Jonathon. The sounds of outside seemed to quieten as Michael sat and watched the peaceful scene.

The old man appeared to be drifting off to a relieving sleep, but the sound of footsteps towards the hut held him in consciousness. Michael watched with curiosity as Ajani's expression changed from relaxed, to alert, and then fearful.

"How are we going in here?"

Michael recognised Ricky's voice, but he kept watching Ajani. "I think we are getting better."

"He is taking on water now," Jonathon said, also concentrating on Ajani. "He needs sleep."

"Well, hopefully he will get a good night's rest," Ricky replied. "We'll need one too—it's going to be a big day tomorrow."

Ricky's words hung in the air as Michael and Jonathon kept watch over Ajani. "Food's ready by the way," Ricky said, breaking the awkward silence as he turned and left the hut.

Ajani spoke softly to Jonathon again, his expression softening once more. Jonathon answered him in soothing tones and offered him another sip of water.

Michael turned off the camera. Following Ricky into the night air, Ajani's reaction stuck in his mind. "He seemed scared of you," he said, struggling to keep up with Ricky's brisk walk towards the vehicles.

"He's had family and friends killed," Ricky replied. "I'm sure you'd be the same"

"But he didn't seem scared of me."

Ricky pursed his lips, as if to prevent what he wanted to say from escaping his mouth. He smiled at Michael. "We've had some good news: the UN are sending in observers to see what's happening here."

"That is good, so what do we do next?"

"I thought you wanted to go home?"

"I do, I want to help out here first."

"We've got a long way to go Michael," Ricky replied. "Getting footage out and the observers in is just the start. We need to stop the pipeline being built or at least change where it's built. To do that, we need something big to attract international pressure."

"What do you mean by 'something big'?"

Ricky again smiled at Michael. They had reached one of the Land Rovers and Ricky took the camera from Michael and began hooking it up to a laptop.

"Tomorrow, we are heading down to Nkumbe. We have heard the army is going to clear it out next, so we need to film them forcing the people off their land."

"But isn't it dangerous for us to be there with the army?"

"The army know how important the pipeline is, Michael. They won't shoot anyone while we are there with cameras rolling," Ricky said. "A foreigner being hurt or killed is the absolute last thing they need."

"What can I do to help?"

"Keep hold of this," Ricky said, unplugging the camera then handing it back to Michael. "Tomorrow's the big one Michael. If we get what we need, the pipeline will have to stop."

"I'll do what I can," Michael replied as Ricky turned his attention to the laptop. He hesitated briefly before turning towards the fire and the food being served.

13

Excitement and nervous energy woke Michael the next morning. The sounds of talking from outside, both in English and the local dialect, told him he was far from the first awake. He rolled himself off the stretcher and stood. As he walked outside and stretched his arms high above his head, he could see that he was in fact one of the last up.

"Just in time, sleepyhead," Beth said with a playful nudge to his ribs. "We're about to have a quick talk about the plan for today." Michael followed Beth towards the pit of last night's now-extinguished fire. A small gathering appeared as they rounded the last of the huts before heading down to the riverbank. A few faces appeared familiar to Michael from the protest in Enugu and it looked as though a few locals had joined. In the middle of the group, deep in conversation with Jonathon, was Ricky. He looked up and, seeing Michael and Beth, quietened the group.

"Now that everyone is here, a few ground rules for today," Ricky started as the group fell silent. "We have had confirmation this morning that the army is moving into Nkumbe to kick out the locals. We have all seen what has happened here over the last couple of days, so we all know how dangerous they can be. Please remember that our job today is to document as much as we can, so we don't want any confrontations. But make sure you don't turn your cameras off. If things get heated, we get out of there and meet back here."

Ricky paused, surveying the group. "Let's not forget why we're here and what these people are going through. Now let's get going."

Michael watched as the Land Rovers were loaded with impressive efficiency. He thought about trying to help, but the BioGuardians moved as though they had done this a hundred times before. He smiled to himself, imagining them practising with Ricky barking orders like a drill sergeant. Before he knew it he was in the back seat of a Land Rover with Ricky at the wheel, Beth beside him, leading the convoy of BioGuardians.

14

Swathes of migrating birds coloured the sky as the BioGuardians left the forest. They followed the road, diving through tall grasses and then along the banks of the river. The sound of the vehicles disturbed the few animals lingering after sunrise. Michael could feel the heat of the early morning sun being reflected off the river.

Slowly the river turned from a muddy brown to a stale grey and, as they rounded an easy bend in the river, Michael could see the reason.

A large pipeline emerged from the grasses and meandered along the far side of the river before turning. It headed for a bridge crossing on which men in fluoro orange overalls were working. A digger on the far side was scrapping and dredging, stirring up turgid grey swirls in the brown water.

The road moved back from the riverside. Large painted wooden stakes appeared between the road and the river, like marching soldiers.

"Marker stakes, for the route of the pipeline," Beth said to Michael, seeing him taking in the scene. "They run straight through the middle of Nkumbe."

"So what was the big plan for today?' Michael asked again, hoping the question wouldn't be brushed aside by Ricky like it was the night before.

"Just keep shooting," Beth replied, much to Michael's disappointment. "The Army aren't known for their PR savvy; I'm sure we'll catch something to help ratchet up the pressure on the oil companies."

"Just keep shooting," Ricky echoed Beth, "whatever happens."

Michael fingered the camera and watched the stakes as they marched on towards Nkumbe.

15

The first of them struck Michael as being a stereotypical African family. A man walked with a large sack of possessions across his back, followed by a woman. His wife, Michael presumed—swathed in colourful cloth with a child sleeping in a sling across her chest. She held more possessions under her arm while a young girl, barefoot, walked beside her, gently holding the tip of her mother's index finger.

But the farther they drove the more they passed. Michael quickly realised that this wasn't an isolated nomadic family on the move. It was a village being driven out.

"What are you waiting for?" Ricky barked from the driver's seat. "Get out the camera." Ricky slowed the vehicle as they weaved through an increasing tide of villagers. As they rose over the crest of a small hill, the village was laid out before them.

Michael filmed what he could of the villagers they were driving past. As they reached the first rows of huts, he turned his attention to the army vehicle blocking their road. They got out of the Land Rover to assess the scene as the rest of the BioGuardians convoy parked behind them. The screaming and crying of a woman grabbed Michael's attention. He tensed up as the soldiers pulling her from her home looked up to see him pointing a camera in their direction.

More soldiers seemed to appear from nowhere, jostling with the BioGuardians, trying to get at anyone holding a camera.

An arm reached around from behind Michael, trying to wrestle the camera from his grasp. He pulled back and fell to the ground with his attacker collapsing down on top of him as a short burst of gunfire rattled across the sky.

A quick silence fell across the melee. The soldier who had fallen on top of Michael sprang to his feet, grabbing a pistol from his belt. He turned and swivelled on his heels, pointing the gun at everyone around him, irrespective of which side they were on. Michael watched, still gripping the camera. The soldier caught sight of someone in the crowd and quickly holstered his gun, standing to an immediate attention.

Between the legs of those around him Michael recognised the waddle he had seen outside Mabolo the previous day, after the crash. Captain Kasolo, his aviator sunglasses gleaming in the sun, stopped in the middle of the group and bellowed "What is going on here? What is the meaning of this?"

"Twice in two days, we must be lucky," Ricky said, stepping forward with a hand outstretched towards Kasolo. Puffing his chest out, Kasolo initially looked at Ricky's hand with disdain. Something caught his eye and he became all too keen to shake hands. The small fold of bills that Ricky had done well to conceal in his palm peeked out over the top of the captain's pudgy fingers as he hastily pocketed the money.

"Mr Ricky, you must surely understand that we have a job to do. The government has decided to resettle these villagers so that our pipeline may proceed."

"We are just here to document the process, Captain," Ricky replied.

"No getting in our way then," Kasolo said, poking a plump finger into Ricky's chest before bellowing at the soldiers, "Get back to work!"

Michael picked himself up from the ground and brushed the red dust from his clothing. The soldiers had dispersed, back to carry out their jobs with more courtesy than before, as they looked around to see if any cameras were on them.

"Are you alright, Michael?" Jonathon asked.

"Yeah," he replied, "I'm fine."

He looked around to see Beth helping a woman with her two children to carry their things as two soldiers looked on, somewhat sheepishly. Kasolo and Ricky were walking off behind one of the vehicles, deep in conversation.

"Let's get to work," Jonathon said, getting a camera out of his bag. Michael checked his to make sure it was still filming and followed Jonathon toward the middle of the village.

The stakes from farther up river were interspersed between the huts. Michael could see them following the road out the other end of the small village. Jonathon's attention was grabbed by something nearby and Michael followed him to a small mud brick hut.

Two soldiers were removing belongings from the hut and placing them into a pile by the road outside. Michael could hear someone sobbing from inside. He moved with Jonathon to get a better view of what was happening as two more soldiers shoved an elderly woman from inside. She collided with Jonathon, spilling her possessions from her hands over the road.

The woman sobbed as she pushed herself from Jonathon and thumped at the two soldiers who had been stacking her items beside the road. As the two struggled to control her an elderly man approached and also began hitting the soldiers. He picked up an old broom and swung it at the soldiers, who called for help from the other two inside the hut.

Michael could sense the situation escalating as another soldier joined in the fracas, while yelling down the street to others. He watched as more villagers joined in, yelling and pushing at the soldiers. Soon a crowd of about twenty villagers had joined the scuffle with the soldiers. Michael backed away, finding refuge against a neighbouring hut, and kept filming.

A ute with four soldiers standing in the back pulled up. One of the soldiers fired three quick shots into the air. Panic set in the crowd as some tried to run away, while others kept trying to attack the soldiers. Michael heard a familiar voice yelling as he saw Beth race to join the scuffle, trying to separate people as a second ute pulled up behind the first.

Three more shots cracked into the air, followed by two further bursts. The crowd screamed and started running in all directions. People were being pushed to the ground as a dust cloud rose, shrouding the group from Michael's view.

As the cloud dispersed in the breeze, Michael could see a small group of villagers picking themselves up from the ground. He saw Beth clutching her ankle and ran to help her. "Are you okay Beth?"

"Yeah, I think so," she replied. "Is anyone else hurt?"

Michael surveyed the scene around him. "I don't think so," he replied as he noticed one person, a man, lying face down and not moving.

"Hello, can you hear me? Are you alright?" he said, shaking the man's shoulder. "Excuse me..." Michael rolled the man over and froze. The man had wounds across his chest, but it was his dead stare that Michael recognised.

"Is he hurt?" Beth asked.

Michael didn't say anything. He kept staring at the face of the dead man.

"Is he...oh my god!" Beth cried. Lying in front of Michael, with three bullet wounds oozing blood across his chest, was Jonathon.

One of the soldiers from the first ute approached cautiously as Beth sobbed and Michael sat, bewildered, staring at Jonathon. Beth's cries brought the attention of one of the villagers who, seeing the body, yelled to the other villagers around her. Screaming broke out and the villagers scrambled to get out of the area as quickly as they could.

Panic set in to the eyes of the soldier who had gotten off the ute. He backed away, slowly at first, before turning and yelling to the rest of the soldiers. They raced back into the utes and sped off. Villagers ran, dropping possessions and tripping over one another. They seemed not to know which direction was the safest to run.

Gunfire cracked further along the row of houses as the panic grew.

"We have to get out of here!" Michael said, grabbing Beth and pulling her to her feet with one hand as he clasped the camera even tighter with his other.

A familiar Land Rover slowed in front of the hut. Michael waved frantically at the driver who he could just make out to be Ricky. "Now!" Michael screamed at Beth. "Let's go." He pulled her to the Land Rover. Further shots sizzled overhead and into the wall of the huts around them.

The sight of a villager being shot and dropping to the ground broke Beth out of her trance. She opened the front door of the Land Rover, climbing in beside Ricky as Michael scrambled his way into the back.

Ricky roared the vehicle along the road and out of the village. Michael watched in horror out the back as their dust rose to cover the chaotic scene with a perverse shade of red.

Villagers were waving frantically at the vehicle, trying to get help as Ricky sped past the final few houses and into the vast plain of tussocks. On the outside of the village the soldiers looked as disorganised as the villagers. Some ran to their vehicles to escape, while others fired shots into the air or through the village at anything that looked like it might be a threat.

Through the chaos, Michael could see Kasolo ducking and waving his hands. He yelled at the police and soldiers around him, pointing at their fleeing vehicle. One of the soldiers' vehicles turned quickly in pursuit of them. The distance between it and the ageing Land Rover started shrinking.

But as they crested a hill and the village dropped from view, the pursuer seemed to stop trying to catch up and pulled off the chase. It turned side on to watch its prey flee. It was as it turned that Michael recognised the design above the rear mud guard. A childish drawing of a lion painted in orange and red and writing underneath, proclaiming "King of the Jungle."

16

The vehicles of the BioGuardians limped back into Mabolo in sporadic drabs. Michael noted that it seemed like no one else had been lost, only Jonathon. A few of the others nursed cuts and bruises. Michael helped Beth from the Land Rover to a stretcher in a hut next to Ajani's.

"It looks like we're reversing roles," Beth said with a wry smile as Michael strapped a chemical ice pack to her ankle. He eased himself back to sit against the wall in the warm glow of the late afternoon sun.

"How do you do this?" he asked. "How do you keep losing friends and stay so positive?"

"It's not easy, I'll say that," Beth replied. "Jonathon is the fourth BioGuardian we've lost in the three years I've been doing this with Ricky. And then there are the people from places like this."

"Don't you worry it could be you one day?"

"It worries me more what would happen if we weren't here. We've stopped other projects and saved the environment for the people who belong to the land. We'll stop this one and save the way of life for Jonathon's family, for Ajani's family too."

Michael sat and let Beth's words sink in.

"What brought you here? To Africa?" Beth asked, breaking the silence.

"I guess I wanted to do something different," Michael replied with a shrug. "I wasn't ready to go to university, to start work..."

"To live a normal boring life?"

"No, not quite, it's just..."

"I know what you mean. We're asked right through our childhood what we want to be when we grow up. Then we grow up and it turns out it's all a crock..."

"I guess so," Michael replied, mulling over Beth's words in his head. "I figured this can't be it. There has to be more than school, then university, then a job. Then I saw the ad for volunteers to teach English and, well, here I am."

"Kudos man, that's a good call."

"I'm not sure my parents would agree with that."

"You should call them," Beth replied. "At least let them know you're alright."

Michael sat and stared into space, running through his hands the strap of the backpack on the ground beside him. He knew his parents would be worried. He knew he should call them. He couldn't bring himself to do it yet. It would mean the end of this. It would mean a faster return to his normal life at home.

"I'm not sure I want to yet," he whispered. "I think I can help out here."

Beth didn't reply and when Michael looked at her he saw she had drifted off to sleep. He felt strange watching her sleep. The usual hum of energy that was Beth had departed for a softer, more feminine glow. Leaning in, he kissed her softly on the forehead. He felt Beth's fingers running softly up the inside of his arm and he pulled back to see that she was looking at him through half-open eyes.

He leaned in again and this time Beth raised her head slightly off the bed to meet his kiss. Beth's lips felt soft but dry and it was Michael who broke the kiss first. "You'd better get some rest," he said, gingerly climbing to his feet, pulling his backpack behind him and returning to the now cool air of the evening.

The village had reduced to a quiet hum. Michael found a secluded spot against a tree. Near the communal fire he reflected on the comfortable life offered to him at home and the struggles of the people in the village. He opened his backpack and took out the camera he had gripped so tightly earlier that day. He might have caught something, he thought, something that might help or make sense of what had happened.

As he watched, the images on the small screen felt so distant now. The look of resignation on those displaced looked like screenshots from an ad for a famine-relief charity rather than the reality he had seen a few hours ago. A small sense of pride came over him as he realised that these were the sorts of images to draw a reaction from the outside world.

The argumentative screams of a woman being forced from her hut brought a sense of dread over Michael. He knew what this scene built up to. He was tempted to stop the video now, but at the same time he felt the need to watch what had happened in the hope of making sense of it.

Sure enough the shooting started. Michael watched the soldiers with their guns pointing skywards let off round after round. From the side of the screen another man with a gun caught his eye. He wasn't wearing a soldier's uniform. He wasn't standing with the soldiers. He wasn't pointing his gun in the air. He was aiming directly at Jonathon. And it was a familiar face holding the gun.

Michael's grief, confusion and dread of watching the video became clouded by anger. He had to watch again as Jonathon's body dropped to the ground, while that face, that vile man, disappeared back into the crowd. This wasn't an accidental shooting. This was cold-blooded murder.

17

Anger and now panic were competing to control Michael. He got to his feet and paced around the fire and up the short hill to the vehicles, adrenaline coursing through him. He forced himself to stop and listen as he heard voices behind one of the four-wheel drives.

He recognised both voices and tossed up the options in his head. He could hear Jonathon's murderer involved in the conversation. Michael could feel his adrenaline surging again, taking over as he rounded the vehicle. Ricky and Peter looked at Michael, guilt seeming to take over their faces as they halted their conversation and stared at Michael.

"Evening Michael," Ricky said, breaking the tense silence.

"What's he doing here?" Michael replied, spitting the words at Ricky.

Peter opened his mouth to reply before Ricky cut him off.

"Peter provides us information on the movements of the army, so we can be prepared."

"To be prepared?" Michael scoffed. "To send Jonathon to his death you mean."

"Calm down Michael," Ricky replied. "We're all sad about Jonathon's death…"

Michael stared at Ricky, while Peter shuffled from foot to foot.

"I think I had better go," Peter said, backing away as Michael and Ricky continued to lock eyes with each other.

"Peter—" Ricky started to say before Michael cut him off.

"Let him go."

Michael waited until he heard Peter's engine start and drive away, crackling the rocks on the road out of the village.

"You knew it was going to happen. You made sure the army was there. You planned for Jonathon to die," Michael hissed. "Why?"

"I'm not sure what you mean," Ricky replied, his voice cracking . "Today was another tragic accident in our fight against the pipeline that is destroying this land."

"Don't lie to me," Michael said. "You and Peter planned this. You knew the army would be there and that things would turn violent. Why did someone have to die?"

"I'm sorry Michael, I don't know what you're talking about. The army were out of control..."

"I saw it! It wasn't the army!" Michael yelled back at Ricky, cutting him off. Michael took a short breath and moved closer to Ricky. He summoned a bricf moment of composure before saying, "I saw you shoot Jonathon."

18

Ricky stepped back and looked quizzically at Michael. "Today's been stressful Michael, you don't want to be throwing accusations around."

Michael closed the gap between them that Ricky had opened. "I got it on camera."

Ricky's expression changed to a combination of guilt and panic. "You can't tell anyone Michael, you have to keep this quiet."

"Why should I?" Michael fired back.

"Because we've almost won," Ricky replied.

"What do you mean?" Michael said, taken aback.

"The evictions today - the displacement of an entire village. Capped off with the death of a local protestor, this is publicity heaven," Ricky said. "The news is already out and we have been frantically working to get videos online. Publicity means action."

"But how does that justify you killing Jonathon?"

"First of all, Peter knew nothing about it and he never will," Ricky replied. "Secondly, it had to be done. We saw a chance to have this thing shut down – for good – and all we had to do was show the government being reckless."

"But what about Jonathon?"

"He's a martyr, the ideal poster boy for us. He died a hero, protecting his land against the evil of the oil companies," Ricky continued. "How are they going to compete against that sort of bad publicity?"

Michael stood, dumbstruck, looking at Ricky. Part of him said that Ricky was right: public pressure would build and maybe, just maybe, something might be done to help these people. But at the same time, he had witnessed a murder and he had proof. He wasn't sure what the right thing to do was. All he knew was that he didn't want to be here any more. "I've got to go," he said, starting to walk back towards the huts.

"Michael," Ricky said, grabbing Michael's shoulder. "You're a long way from home. Accidents happen around here all the time. Keep your mouth shut and I'm sure you'll be safe."

Michael absorbed Ricky's words, shook himself free of the grip on his shoulder and headed back to the hut where Beth was fast asleep.

He took the camera out of his bag once more, replacing the memory card with a blank one and putting the card with the footage of Jonathon's murder down his sock. He lay down on a stretcher and watched the glimpse of night sky he could see through the doorway, knowing that sleep would not come easily tonight.

19

The first sign of morning light drew Michael from his bed. He wasn't sure how much sleep he had been able to get last night, if any at all. He began packing his possessions into his pack, planning how to leave the camp.

"What are you doing?" Beth's voice sounded hoarse as she roused from a deep sleep.

"Nothing," Michael replied. "Go back to sleep."

"Are you packing? Where are you going?" Beth sounded more awake, more urgent this time.

"I've got to get out of here," Michael replied, "I need to get home."

"And you weren't even going to say goodbye?" The tone of Beth's voice changed, sounding more concerned.

"What's wrong Michael?"

"I've got to go, OK?"

"Michael…" Beth said, putting her hand on his arm.

Michael looked at her. There was something pleading in her eyes.

"I saw something," he said, in almost a whisper. "Something I shouldn't have."

"What do you mean?"

"Jonathon. His death." Michael held onto the next few words, contemplating what would happen when he let them out of his mouth.

"It wasn't the army's fault. Ricky shot him."

Beth took her hand from Michael's arm. "No, that can't be right."

"I saw it Beth, I caught it on camera."

"No, I still can't believe it. Have you asked him about it? Maybe there is some other explanation."

"He doesn't deny it," Michael replied, "in fact he planned it."

Beth retreated further back onto her stretcher. "Be careful what you're saying Michael. I don't think that's right," she said as tears began to build in her eyes.

"Ricky wanted a martyr," Michael said, "someone to die for the cause. He thinks that a death like this will put pressure on the companies to stop the pipeline's route through these villages."

Michael watched Beth for a reaction. She seemed to be taking in everything he had said and weighing it up.

"Maybe he's got a point?" Beth said.

Michael sat back in shock. "You can't be serious"

"It's terrible what happened, I know, but what if that one death can stop hundreds more?" Beth said. "What if that one death saves the villages and moves or even stops the pipeline?"

Michael looked at her, mouth open, aghast at what she was saying.

"Think about it Michael. What's happening here is bigger than any single one of us. What if we could help protect the future of these people?"

It horrified Michael that someone could think this way, but at the same time, Beth had a point. He subconsciously fumbled with the memory card in his sock. If that video ever got out then it would be the end of the BioGuardians' credibility and would guarantee the progress of the pipeline.

But if he kept it quiet, he thought, the villages might be saved – but what about justice for Jonathon and, more importantly, what if Ricky did it again?

The silence between Beth and Michael was broken by a growing excitement outside. They could hear someone yelling for everyone to gather round. They left their hut and headed to where a small gathering of BioGuardians and villagers was growing.

As they neared the group, Michael could see Ricky was at the centre, telling those around him to quieten down.

"We've had some big news come through overnight." he said. "AAP have announced construction of the pipeline has been suspended." A cheer rippled across the crowd, though Michael found himself unsure of how to take the news.

"Pending an inquiry into the tragic death of our good friend Jonathon, they are going to move the path of the pipeline. Or even stop the construction completely."

Michael backed away from the group, until he felt a hand on his shoulder. "See," Beth whispered, "Jonathon's death might have helped us." He turned and looked her in the eye, feeling like he no longer recognised who Beth was.

"I can't be here anymore," he said.

"What about me?" Beth replied. "Won't you stay for me?"

"I'm sorry Beth. I want to help you, to help these people, but not like this."

"At least stay for breakfast," she replied, "then I'll help get you on your way."

Michael looked at Beth, "thanks" the only word he could muster. Beth pulled him and kissed him softly on the cheek before taking his hand and leading them to the dining area.

20

Michael ate more out of necessity than any particular desire or hunger. He was exhausted and confused, but at least Beth's offer to get him home made him feel slightly less uneasy. Beth, sitting beside him, had been quiet and her silence spoke more to him than any of the conversations they had had over the last few days.

"I don't think I'm going to tell anyone, Beth," he said, trying to break the silence.

"Whatever you do, you need to be able to live with it, not any of us," Beth replied. "I'm sure you'll do the right thing."

"I'm not even sure I know what the right thing is. Yes, it's great that these villages may have been saved, but Jonathon was murdered. How do I reconcile that with myself?"

Beth didn't reply. She finished her food and took Michael's now empty plate, putting it on the pile of dirty dishes. "Come on then, let's get you home."

They walked in silence back towards their hut, where flickers of movement inside caused Michael to pick up pace. He could see his backpack on the ground, with two BioGuardians rummaging through his belongings. "Hey!" he shouted at them. "What are you doing?"

The two turned, dropping Michael's backpack on the floor of the hut. Neither of them spoke as Ricky, who Michael hadn't been able to see in the shadows of the hut, stepped out.

"Where is it Michael?"

"Where's what?" Michael replied, knowing full well what he was after.

"The memory card Michael. We can't trust you with it, not when we're this close."

"It's in a safe place," Michael said, "and I'm going to make sure it stays safe."

"What are you going to do with it?" Ricky asked.

"I'm not sure, I really don't know."

Ricky grabbed Michael by his shirt and pulled him into the hut, shoving him against a wall. Michael tried to push free, but Ricky was too strong for him. "Where is it? I'm not playing now," Ricky hissed.

Michael looked at the desperation in Ricky's eyes and thought about what he had said to him the night before. "Let Beth take me to the border," he said, voice quivering, "and I'll give it to her."

"Ricky!" Beth called from outside, speaking up for the first time since they had returned to the hut. "I think you had better see this."

"Not now," Ricky replied. "We're busy."

"No, Ricky, I *really* think you need to see this."

"What?" Ricky snapped, dragging Michael back outside.

Michael could feel the grip on his shirt loosen as he stumbled behind Ricky outside the hut. As he looked up he could see the reason why. Police vehicles had materialised in the camp and the BioGuardians were being rounded up. Walking towards the hut, with an angry swagger, was Captain Kasolo.

21

"Kasolo!" Ricky called through a forced smile. "Good to see you, how can we help you today?"

Captain Kasolo didn't respond; he instead walked straight up to Ricky, raised his baton above his head and struck Ricky across the cheek. Ricky fell to the ground and Kasolo rained down several more blows on his back and shoulders.

"You scum!" Kasolo screamed at Ricky. "We had an agreement and you screwed it up! Who is going to pay me my oil money now!"

"Stop it!" Beth yelled as Kasolo again belted Ricky. Michael grabbed her arm as she tried to intervene and the distraction allowed Ricky to get to his feet and scramble away from Kasolo.

Ricky stumbled and scrambled away through a gap between two of the huts. Furious, Kasolo yelled incoherently towards the other officers who were standing guard around the remaining BioGuardians.

"We need to get out of here Beth," Michael whispered as Kasolo swung around to look at them.

"You!" he bellowed, pointing at Beth. "This is your fault." Kasolo drew his pistol and aimed it towards Beth as Michael pulled her towards the Land Rovers. Michael winced as a couple of shots whizzed past them.

The shots caused panic in the group of BioGuardians, who began scrambling for cover. Further shots cracked into the air from Kasolo and the rest of the police as the village descended into chaos.

Michael pulled Beth into shelter behind one of the Land Rovers. Edging the door open, he could see the keys in the ignition. He pulled Beth to her feet as two more shots fizzed past before a third sound, a sickening dull thud, caught Michael's attention. Beth collapsed against Michael with a whimper.

Fear gripped Michael. He pulled Beth back up and pushed her into the Land Rover, making just enough room for himself to follow along behind and scramble into the driver's seat.

It wasn't until he turned the key to start the vehicle that he noticed the sticky red blood smeared across his hand. He threw the vehicle into gear and reached across to Beth, who hadn't moved since they had clambered inside. "Beth," he cried at her, "wake up Beth!"

He shook her with one hand, while steering erratically up the narrow jungle path with the other. Beth groaned while Michael shook her again, trying to raise some sort of response from her. Michael put both hands on the wheel as they bounced along the bumpy road through the shadows of the trees. He drove as fast as he could, while trying to watch Beth for some sign that she was alright.

The jungle retreated away from the road, to Michael's relief, and they sped out along a straightening road across tussocked plains. The direct sunlight now on them allowed Michael to see that Beth was bleeding from her lower back. She moaned again, trailing off to a whimper. Michael studied the rear-vision mirror for a few brief moments. When he was sure there was no one following behind them, he pulled off the track and behind a small group of trees and scrub, hiding from the road as best he could.

The trees provided some shade as Michael laid a blanket, grabbed a first-aid kit from the Land Rover and helped Beth from the vehicle. She still hadn't spoken, but he could feel her trying to move with him, straining as she lay down on the blanket.

He lifted her blood-soaked shirt and could just make out the bullet wound. Pulsing blood oozed out and ran down her side, soaking into the blanket. Wiping away what blood he could, Michael pressed a gauze square from the first-aid kit hard against Beth, to which she let out a loud groan of pain.

The gauze quickly became soaked with blood as Michael looked for something else to help stem the bleeding. He tore a piece from the blanket, folding it into a square and pushing it into the wound, trying to get enough pressure on to stop the flow.

"Michael," Beth groaned, able to speak weakly through gritted teeth, "get us to the ranger station. Peter will be able to help us."

"You're going to be OK Beth," Michael replied, trying to convince himself that it was true. He pulled a roll of tape from the kit and strapped the already soaked blanket square against Beth. With a grunt he lifted her back into the Land Rover.

"You're going to be fine," he repeated, brushing a wisp of hair away from her eyes.

Beth looked back at him and whispered, "Thank you Michael. You're a brave man."

Michael nudged the door closed and returned to the driver's seat. Crawling at first back to the roadside, when he was sure they were alone on the road, he pushed the Land Rover as fast it would go. Trailing a cloud of dust, they raced back towards the ranger station at the edge of the Korup National Park.

22

"Hold on, Beth," Michael said, as he finally pulled into the ranger station. Pulling Beth from her seat, he saw Peter come rushing out.

"Michael," he called, "what happened?"

"The police," Michael replied. "They shot her."

They carried Beth inside, slipping in and out of consciousness, clearing a space on the floor to lay her down.

Beth softly placed her hand on Michael as he lifted the makeshift bandage away from her wound. Her touch felt cold and weak as blood continued to ooze.

He wiped it away with wet cloths. Peter rolled a towel and placed it under Beth's head before retrieving the station's first-aid kit and offering it to Michael.

Michael kept working on the wound, wiping and compressing, as Peter knelt beside Beth's head, dabbing her brow with a damp cloth.

"Hold on," Michael kept whispering. "Hold on Beth. I need you."

Slowly, the pulsing of blood reduced and Michael wouldn't let his focus move from trying to stop the bleeding.

Beth's hand fell away from Michael as he once again changed the swab he was holding against her.

The bleeding had finally stopped.

With some relief, Michael looked towards Peter, who looked back with sadness in his eyes.

"I'm sorry Michael," he whispered. "She's gone."

23

Michael and Peter both jumped as someone banged on the door of the ranger station. Still in shock, and crouched over Beth's body, Peter had to pull Michael away from her and towards the room at the back.

"Peter, thank god!" Michael heard through the door, recognising Ricky's drawl. "They're after me, you have to help..." As Ricky's voice cut off, Michael knew that he had seen Beth's body. He opened the door and stepped out to see Ricky kneeling over her.

"What happened?" Ricky asked, looking in shock at Michael.

"What do you mean 'what happened'?" Michael replied hoarsely, tears streaming down his face. "This is your fault." He dragged Ricky to his feet and pushed him against the wall. "First you kill Jonathon and now Beth is dead, both because of your stupid plan to have a martyr!"

"What do you mean?" Peter asked, trying to get between Ricky and an increasingly aggressive Michael.

"It wasn't the army at all. Ricky was shooting into the crowd, trying to attract outside attention to himself," Michael replied, almost spitting each word out.

"Is this true?" Peter asked, shifting his attention to Ricky, who could only look at the ground.

"You bastard!" Peter roared, pushing Michael out of the way and shoving Ricky harder against the wall. He lifted him to the point where only the tips of his toes touched the ground.

Michael thought how Ricky looked genuinely fearful for the first time since he challenged him about shooting Jonathon. "I got it on camera," he said to Peter. "We can hand it to the authorities, make him pay for what he has done."

"Think about this Peter," Ricky cut in with a gasp. "The pipeline, it is stopped now and worst-case scenario, it will go around the villages. Your lands are protected thanks to the sacrifice Jonathon made."

Peter released his grip on Ricky, starting to turn away before swinging back around and punching Ricky with a cracking blow to his face. Michael stood and watched, feeling no sympathy at all as Ricky slid to the ground.

"What do we do?" Michael asked Peter softly, putting his arm around the ranger's shoulders as Peter cupped his hands across his face.

"He's right," Peter said, snorting in a breath. Michael could see his eyes had reddened with tears of what was either anger, sadness or a combination of both.

"The piece of scum is right," he continued. "We turn him in, the pipeline is back on track, we don't and he gets away with murder."

"We should do the right thing for Jonathon," Michael replied. "If we turn him in, we get justice for Jonathon and you never know, the publicity out there might be enough to sway the oil companies anyway..."

"What a load of bull," Ricky muttered from the floor. "Release that tape and we look like a bunch of raving lunatics and the pipeline goes ahead as planned."

The three exchanged uneasy glances as Ricky pulled himself up from the floor. "The one thing I know is that we need to get out of here," he said. "Kasolo and his goons will be looking for us."

"I think you might be too late," Peter replied, glancing out the window. Michael and Ricky looked at each other as they heard vehicles pulling up outside and car doors slamming closed. Kasolo had arrived.

24

"Hide in that cupboard!" whispered Peter, nodding at a bulky, beaten-up, two-door metal locker at the back of the room.

"What about hiding in the back room?" Michael asked.

"No," Ricky cut in. "Our vehicles are outside, they'll search the place. We need to hide as best we can." He opened the locker and pushed aside a bunch of hanging clothes. "In you get, slide across to the far side," he said to Michael.

The hanging clothes gave some camouflage. They also served to increase the heat inside the locker as Ricky and Michael squeezed in behind them. A small hole near the top of one of the doors allowed Michael to see out. He watched as Peter waited for Ricky to close the locker, before opening the front door of the ranger station.

"Captain Kasolo, sir, how wonderful to have your presence," Peter called. Michael watched Kasolo waddle into the ranger station, elbowing past Peter.

"Where are they?" he snapped, wheezing as he looked up at Peter.

"Well, the girl, she is dead," Peter replied, nodding to Beth's body on the floor. "She is the only one I have seen."

Kasolo wiped sweat from his brow and surveyed the room. "I think you are lying, ranger," he said, turning back to face Peter. "There are two vehicles outside that do not belong to you. Are you trying to say that one girl can drive two cars?"

Michael felt fear in the pit of his stomach. "Take this," Ricky whispered to him. Michael felt for what Ricky was offering in the stuffy darkness.

He recognised the feel of a camera being pushed into his hand. "You seem to be very good at capturing things on film, so remember to keep quiet and keep shooting," Ricky continued.

Through the gap in the locker Michael continued to spy on Kasolo. He slowly and quietly raised the camera to the narrow gap and pushed record as Kasolo barked clipped words at someone outside.

Two more burly men in police uniforms came through the door and pushed Peter against the wall. "I will ask you once more: where are they?" Kasolo said.

"Remember what I told you," Ricky whispered to Michael, before opening the door on his side of the locker and stepping out. "I'm here, Kasolo."

Kasolo spun around and eyed Ricky up and down. "Check the other rooms," he barked at his two assistants.

Michael's pulse raced and he felt sweat rolling off his forehead. He sunk as far back as he could into the locker, away from the doors, keeping the camera up to the hole he had been spying through. He could hear Kasolo's men rummaging in the back room.

He held his breath and urged himself to be as silent as possible. One of the men emerged and glanced at the locker, before moving on to open the other cupboards in the room.

"It's just me here," Ricky said as Kasolo's men returned and nodded in agreement with Ricky's assertion. "I don't know where the other guy is. I last saw him in Mabolo."

Michael watched the small screen on the back of the camera as Kasolo appeared to tense up. He put his hand on top of the baton tucked through his belt loop, fingering the grip as he looked around the room.

With a yell of frustration he pulled the baton out, spun with surprising agility, and cracked it across the side of Ricky's head. The sickening sound made Michael flinch. Ricky stumbled, trying to balance himself against the wall, before falling to the floor. Kasolo raised his baton above his head and crashed it down, seemingly not caring where he hit Ricky, just that he could hit him with as much force as possible.

Kasolo seemed to pull up with exhaustion while Ricky groaned on the floor. "Outside," Kasolo said to his men, before delivering a swift kick to Ricky's stomach. Michael watched as the men grabbed an arm each and dragged Ricky out the front door and out of sight.

Unsure of what to do, Michael looked at Peter who, seemingly sensing Michael's gaze, held up his hand, indicating for him to wait. Peter stared at the floor, shuffling his feet as if he knew exactly what was coming.

Michael jumped at the first gunshot, but the second seemed somewhat expected. He looked again towards Peter who had dropped his hand to his side. Michael listened to the sound of vehicles starting outside and waited until their rumble had dissipated into the distance. Peter didn't look at him as he slid out of the locker, his hair matted against his forehead with sweat.

He walked slowly past Peter and edged closer to the door. Ricky's feet soon came into view and as Michael shuffled further out, he could see the rest of Ricky, lying awkwardly on the dirt in a pool of drying blood.

Feeling faint and nauseous, he gripped against the door frame as he slid to the floor. He could feel tears streaming down his face and the world around him started to spin. Michael almost felt relief for a split second before he fainted against the wall.

25

The warmth of the late afternoon sun on his face woke Michael and he took a few moments to take in his surroundings. He was no longer at the ranger station. He was sitting in the passenger seat of a vehicle parked near a languid, green-brown river. Forest greeted the river on the far side and he could make out a small, single-lane bridge crossing the river and cutting its way through the trees. On the closer side the banks were lightly grassed and littered with small piles of rocks.

Michael could make out Peter, surrounded by piles of red dirt, as he dug a large hole. Alongside was a second hole of similar size to what Peter was currently digging. It didn't take Michael very long to work out that Peter was digging two graves. He shuffled around in his seat. Looking in the back of the vehicle he saw two long objects wrapped in white sheeting, one of which had a brownish-red stain drying in the sun.

Rubbing his eyes, Michael eased himself off the passenger seat and balanced against the open door. "Do you need a hand?" he called to Peter.

"No. And you should be resting," Peter replied as he stopped digging and walked to the vehicle.

"I'm fine," Michael replied, rocking unsteadily on his feet. "Where are we?"

"That," Peter said, pointing across the river, "is the border to Nigeria. We're going to get you home."

Michael eased himself back to perch against the edge of the seat. "Thank you Peter," he said softly. "And what about you?"

Peter leaned on his spade like a crutch as he spoke. "I'll be fine. Kasolo doesn't know I helped you." He paused briefly, looking around and taking a slow breath. "This is my land. I grew up here. I'll die here. If I am helping my people, I'm serving my purpose in life."

Michael stood in silence for a few moments, trying to absorb everything that had happened over the last few days. He sighed softly as Peter spoke again. "Come Michael, we need to finish this job."

Michael absentmindedly ran his finger along the sun-warmed metal and across the "King of the Jungle" painting as they walked to the back of the vehicle in silence.

Michael could tell instinctively that the first sheet-wrapped body they carried was Ricky. He felt solid and heavy, almost daring Michael to drop him.

The heat of the sun had dwindled now, but he broke into a sweat from the weight of the body. Awkwardly, they lay him into one of the graves Peter had dug.

Carrying Ricky's body had felt cold, mechanical, but Michael felt a sense of dread as they turned to return to the vehicle.

He stopped briefly—Beth's sheet-wrapped form still exuded the warmth of her spirit. Michael felt tears softly rolling down his cheeks as they carried her and gently lay her in the warm red earth.

Michael reached for a small white daisy poking out from between two rocks beside the graves. He pulled it from the ground and laid it on Beth's chest, caressing the top of her head.

They stood for a brief moment in silence in front of both graves. Peter moved away first, silently collecting his spade and slowly filling in the graves, Ricky's first.

Michael, moving with the same quietness, retrieved a second spade form the back of the vehicle and steadily pushed the red earth into the holes.

Rested on his spade, exhausted, Michael watched Peter collecting large stones, placing them on top of the graves they had just filled. Michael did the same. They rolled bigger rocks into place before shovelling smaller rocks and stones on top until there was a pile covering the length of each grave. A low growl from the far riverbank reminded Michael why such a step was necessary.

Sharing a swig of water from Peter's canteen, they packed their spades back into the vehicle. They took a moment to reflect, as the sun started to disappear behind the tree tops.

"I want to thank you," Peter said. "I told you to go, but you stayed to help my people."

Michael stayed quiet. He had always felt awkward receiving any sort of praise and this felt particularly hard, given what they had just done.

"There is one more thing we need you to do," Peter continued. Michael looked and saw that Peter was holding the camera that Michael had used at the ranger station.

"Of course," Michael replied, taking the camera and shrinking back against the vehicle as he heard an engine near the bridge on the other side of the river. He watched as a white ute emerged from the shadows and stopped on the Nigerian side of the river.

"Your ride is here," Peter said, waving to the vehicle. "Harry is a friend in the Nigerian Ranger Service. He will take you to your embassy in Abuja. They will be able to help you get home."

"I don't know how to thank you Peter," Michael said.

"Yes, you do," Peter replied, tapping the top of the camera. "Good luck Michael."

Walking onto the bridge, Michael felt a confusing sense of relief and sadness come over him. He stopped in the middle of the bridge to look back.

Saying a silent prayer, he took a last look at the two graves near the edge of the river. He reached into his sock and pulling out the memory card of Jonathon's death. "I'm going to do the right thing Beth," he said to himself as he tossed the memory card into the river. He walked the rest of the way across the bridge, cradling the camera, the evidence against Kasolo, like a precious jewel.

26

Sitting at home, Michael had finally escaped the constant presence of his mother checking his wellbeing. Her questions had come thick and fast. The one he reflected on most was one that his mother had probably meant as a throwaway comment: "Did you find yourself?"

Michael turned on the television in time for the evening news.

"And now to international news, where Cameroon officials today arrested three police officers for murder, including Captain Kasolo, the officer seen beating well-known environmental protestor Ricky Benson in footage uploaded anonymously to the internet last week. All Africa Petroleum, the company Benson was protesting against, have released a statement welcoming the arrests and confirming plans to move the route of their oil pipeline currently under construction through Chad and Cameroon..."

Moving to his desk, he let the news become white noise in the background. A stack of applications to join environmental groups was on his desk and Michael reflected on his new calling. He took a brief moment to remind himself of what was at stake as he looked at the photo of Beth he had clipped from the newspaper. Her smile beamed from the page under the headline "Environmentalists pay the ultimate price".

-//-